YOU AND YOUR CHILD
PAINT FUN

Ray Gibson

Illustrated by Sue Stitt,
Simone Wood and Graham Round

Designed by Lindy Dark

Edited by Paula Borton

Series editors: Robyn Gee and Jenny Tyler

Photography by John Bellenis

Children are fascinated by the feel and colour of paint and, with this book, adults and children can have fun exploring together a range of paint techniques and materials. All the projects are simple yet stimulating, ensuring hours of amusement while providing the context for many learning opportunities.

First published in 1992 by Usborne Publishing Ltd, Usborne House, 83-85 Saffron Hill, London EC1N 8RT, England. Copyright © 1992 Usborne Publishing Ltd. The name Usborne and the device ⏚ are Trade Marks of Usborne Publishing Ltd.

W9-BXH-469

Munching monster

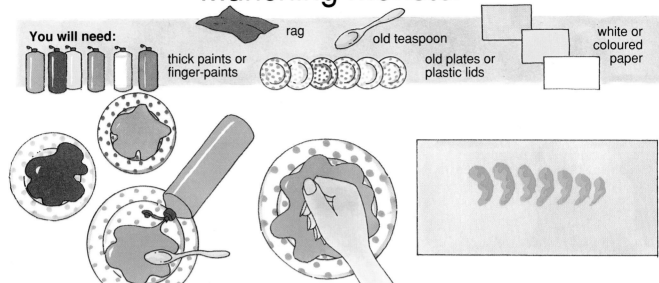

You will need:

thick paints or finger-paints

rag

old teaspoon

old plates or plastic lids

white or coloured paper

Pour paint onto old plates. Spread the paint with a teaspoon.

Clench your hand into a fist and press, as shown, into the paint. Rock your hand from side to side making sure it is well coated with paint.

Press the side of your fist onto a sheet of paper, then lift it off. Repeat the prints in a curved line to make a body.

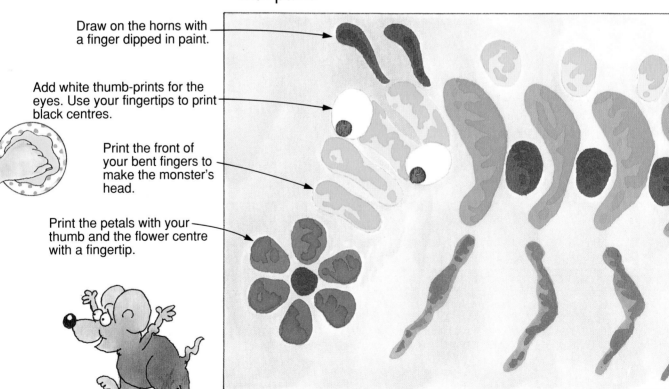

Draw on the horns with a finger dipped in paint.

Add white thumb-prints for the eyes. Use your fingertips to print black centres.

Print the front of your bent fingers to make the monster's head.

Print the petals with your thumb and the flower centre with a fingertip.

Other ideas

Bees on flowers

On yellow paper, use the front of your bent fingers to print black bees' bodies. Allow the bodies to dry and add white thumb-print wings. With a fine paintbrush, draw in the antennae. Print some big bright flowers.

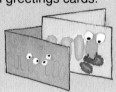

Big-eyed bugs

Print the bugs with the front of your clenched fingers. Finger print the eyes. Make your own greetings cards.

Spot-and-wipe dragonflies

Dip a finger into thick paint and then press onto paper. Pull the paint into a tail and then lift off quickly. Add some wings with the side of your little finger and draw in the antennae.

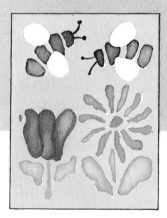

Wipe your hands with a rag in between colours.

Hints

•Before you start, print various parts of your hand to find all the different shapes you can make.

•Change hands to make 'side of the fist' prints curve in the opposite direction.

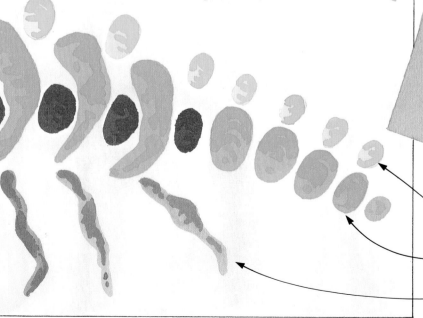

Print some decorations with your fingers and thumbs.

Finger print the tail.

For the legs, print the side of your little finger.

3

Rainbow fish

You will need: large sheets of white paper · small household paintbrush · pot of water · ready-mix paints (including blue, green and white) · pencil · egg box · 2 saucers · round-ended scissors

Sea

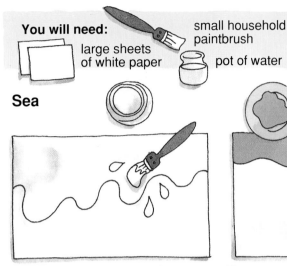

Using a household paintbrush, quickly paint a sheet of paper with water.

Pour green paint onto a saucer. Paint a wavy green line across the top of the wet paper. Rinse your brush.

Pour blue paint onto another saucer. Paint a wavy blue line under the green. Repeat this until you reach the bottom of the sheet. Leave it to dry.

Fish

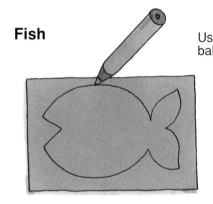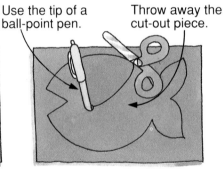

Use the tip of a ball-point pen.

Throw away the cut-out piece.

Draw a fat fish shape onto a piece of thin cardboard. Leave a wide edge.

Poke a hole in the fish. Insert the scissors into the hole. Cut to the outside edge, and then around the fish shape.

Lightly tape the stencil onto a white piece of paper.

Other fish ideas

Dab on stripes.

Print the corner of the sponge.

Print the edge of the sponge.

Fold the sponge so the edge forms a V shape, and use it to print.

4

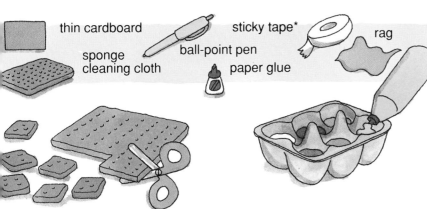

thin cardboard

sponge
cleaning cloth

ball-point pen

sticky tape*

paper glue

rag

Cut at least 6 squares, about 3cm by 3cm (1in by 1in), from a sponge cloth.

Squeeze some paint into the holes of an empty egg box.

Other ideas

Birds in a tree

Paint a watery blue sky and a tree. Make bird shapes in the same way as the fish. Sit your birds on the tree.

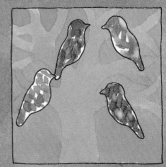

Tulips

Make tulip shapes and glue them onto a grassy background. Draw in the stems and leaves.

Dip a piece of sponge into the paint and dab lightly over the stencil.

Wipe the stencil both sides with a rag before making more fish shapes.

Print bubbles by dipping the end of a pencil into white paint.

Dip the end of a pencil into black paint and print eyes.

When the fish are dry, cut them out and glue them

clear tape or cellophane tape (U.S.)

to the background. Sponge print sand and seaweed.

5

Surprise patterns

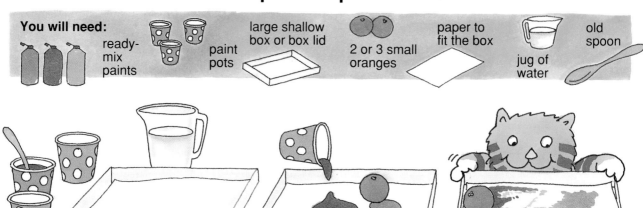

You will need: ready-mix paints · paint pots · large shallow box or box lid · 2 or 3 small oranges · paper to fit the box · jug of water · old spoon

In the paint pots, mix each paint with a little water. Lay a sheet of paper inside a large shallow box.

Pour blobs of paint onto the paper and place two or three oranges into the box.

Tilt the box so that the oranges roll around, mixing and spreading the paint into patterns.

Hints

• If you don't have any oranges use medium-sized balls.

• The oranges will rinse off easily after use and may safely be eaten.

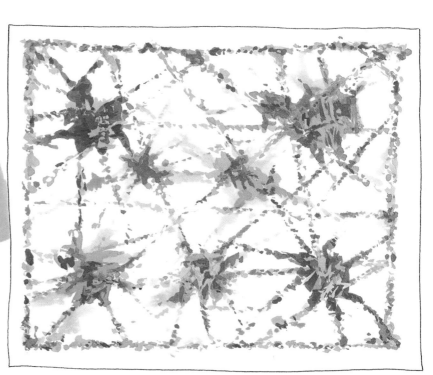

Remove the oranges. Now watch the colours change and merge as they dry. You could try this with undiluted paint.

Beautiful butterfly

You will need:

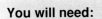 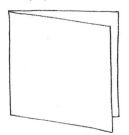 sheet of pale paper

 sheet of black paper

ready-mix paints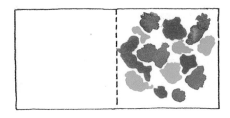

glue

round-ended scissors

pencil

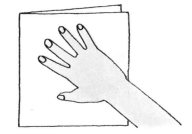

Fold a sheet of pale paper in half and crease it in the middle.

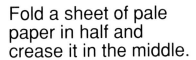

Open out the paper and squeeze blobs of paint onto one side.

Refold the paper and smooth it gently to spread the paint.

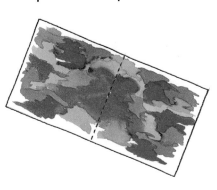

Open it out again and see your pattern. Leave the paint to dry.

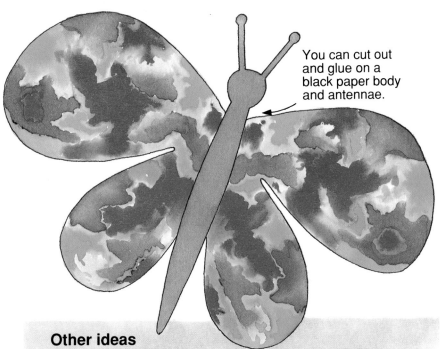

You can cut out and glue on a black paper body and antennae.

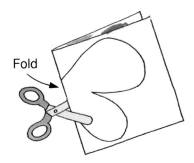

Fold

When dry, fold the paper and draw half a butterfly shape. Cut the shape out leaving the paper joined at the fold. Then open it out.

Other ideas

String print

Dip a length of string in paint and coil it onto one half of a sheet of paper. Fold the paper and smooth it down. Open it out and remove the string to reveal a pattern.

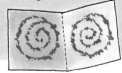

Lots of butterflies

Fold the paper so the long edges meet. You can then draw and cut out lots of butterflies along the same fold.

7

Fire! Fire!

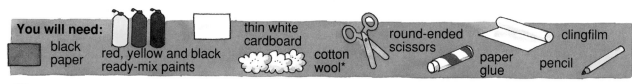

You will need: black paper, red, yellow and black ready-mix paints, thin white cardboard, cotton wool*, round-ended scissors, paper glue, clingfilm, pencil

Squeeze red and yellow paint in wiggly lines on the centre of a piece of cardboard. Add a few squirts of black paint.

Lay a sheet of clingfilm completely over the cardboard. Dab the surface with cotton wool to spread and mix the colours.

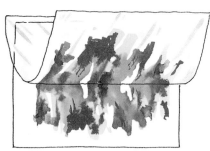

Peel off the clingfilm from the bottom to the top. The paint will be pulled into flames.

Press wisps of cotton wool onto the wet paint for the smoke.

Using black paper, cut out and glue on a fire engine and other objects.

Cut doors and windows to show flames.

Hints

●Microwave clingfilm is firm and easy to handle. You could tape down the corners while you work.

●You can also make a print by pressing the peeled-off clingfilm onto a fresh piece of paper.

Arctic scene

Use cold colours such as blue, green, black and white to make an iceberg picture. Add cut-out polar bears, walruses and whales.

8   *cotton (U.S.)

Stained glass shapes

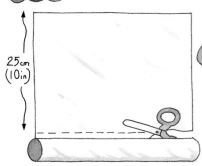

25cm (10in)

Cut a piece of clingfilm about 25cm (10in) long. Lay it on a flat surface and smooth out any wrinkles.

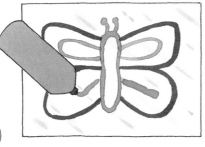

Squeeze paint thinly onto the clingfilm to make a shape. Leave a wide margin. Use lots of colours.

Carefully lay a second piece of clingfilm on top of the painted piece. Press down the edges.

Using your fingers, spread and smooth the paint.

Hints

- Shake the paint bottles well before you begin.

- This project does not work so well with ordinary clingfilm.

- Be careful not to use too much paint as it will sink to the bottom of your picture.

Press your clingfilm picture onto a window. Firmly dab the paint with your finger and see the light shine through the colours. Tape the bottom of the clingfilm to prevent any drips.

Wallpaper print

 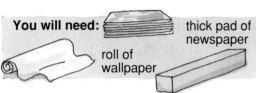

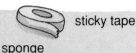
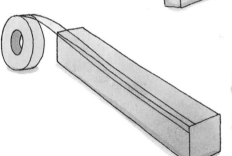

Close the lid of a long narrow box. Use sticky tape to seal the lid and cover any cutting edges.

Cut a strip of sponge cloth the same width as the box.

Snip the strips into rectangles of various sizes. Cut the rectangles into different shapes, saving the leftover pieces.

Spread PVA glue along the top of the box.

Press your sponge shapes into the glue. Use small leftover pieces in the gaps. Allow the glue to dry.

Fold a piece of cloth so it is a little longer and wider than the box. Place the cloth on a thick pad of newspaper.

Some printing ideas

Try printing with different kinds of cloth, such as corduroy, coarse wool and felt.

Print vegetables cut in half, or cut shapes into a halved potato.

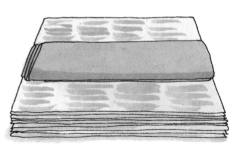

See the shapes you can get by printing with pasta, pencil ends, crumpled paper, coiled playdough, corrugated cardboard and leaves.

PVA glue*
glue spreader
jug of water
piece of cloth
old or plastic teaspoon
ready-mix paint

Hints

• If you don't have any wallpaper use a large piece of paper or used computer paper.

• Cut centres out of the sponge shapes by folding them in half and snipping out the middles.

Moisten the cloth with a little water. Then squirt the paint, as shown, and spread it with the back of a spoon.

Press the box firmly into the paint and rock it from side to side to cover the sponges evenly.

Firmly press the box onto the wrong side of a piece of wallpaper. Then lift it off to leave a print.

Other ideas

Print a border on a paper tablecloth.

Print on tissue paper to make colourful wrapping paper.

Decorate a box with wallpaper prints to make a room for your toys.

Use two or more boxes to make colourful prints.

Continue to print down the length of the paper. You can try turning the box around to make a different print.

*See Parents' notes for U.S.

11

Giant sunflower

 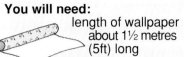

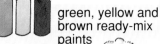

Weigh down corners if the paper curls.

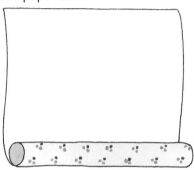

Put one hand inside the boot while painting.

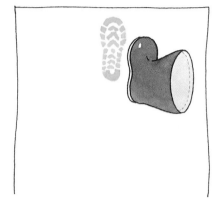

Lay a length of wallpaper on a long table or a washable floor.

Pour some yellow paint into a saucer. Now paint the sole of the larger wellington boot using a household paintbrush.

Press the boot firmly onto the top centre of the paper. Lift off to leave a print of the first petal.

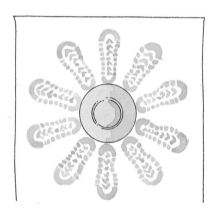

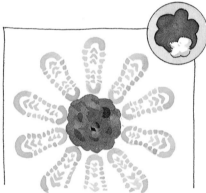

Rinse your brush.

Place a clean saucer directly beneath the petal. Using the saucer as a guide print a circle of petals, as shown. Repaint the sole of the boot before each print.

Remove the saucer and pour some brown paint onto it. Using a piece of cotton wool dab on a brown centre.

For the stem, pour some green paint onto a saucer. Roll up a newspaper and paint one side of it green.

Hints

- If your yellow is too pale to print well, mix in a little red paint.

- Rock the boot from side to side, and press the toe end down to achieve an even print.

- To clean the boots, wash them under a running cold tap and stand them on newspaper until dry.

pot of water

 2 small wellington boots with patterned soles - in different sizes if possible

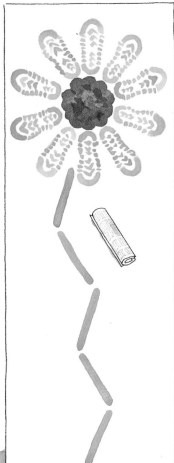

Use the painted newspaper to print a stem down the length of the paper. Try not to print a straight line.

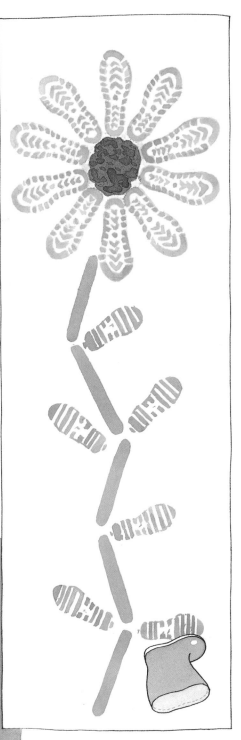

Other ideas

Dragonfly
Print a body and large head using cotton wool dipped in paint. Print wings using large and small boots

Fish
Print a body and paint on a tail and fins.

Bugs
Print the body and add on eyes and antennae.

For the leaves, paint the sole of a smaller boot green. Use it to print leaves along the stem, as shown.

13

Rainbow string print

You will need: string, cardboard tube, sticky tape, round-ended scissors, old newspaper, cleaning cloth or rag, jug of water, plastic teaspoon, large sheets of paper

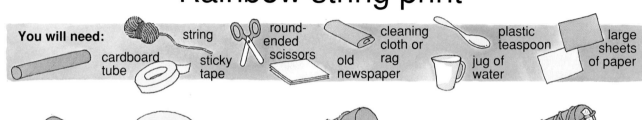

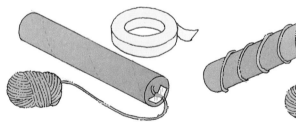

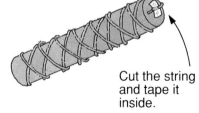

Cut the string and tape it inside.

Tape the loose end of some string onto the inside of a cardboard tube.

Wrap the string along the tube.

Make criss-cross patterns by winding the string up and down the length of the tube.

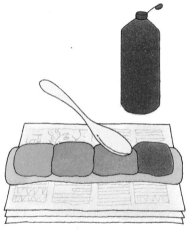

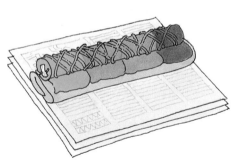

Fold a rag or cleaning cloth into a rectangle. Lay it on a thick pad of newspaper. Add a few drops of water to the cloth and let it soak in.

Pour four colours onto the cloth, as shown. Spread the paints with the back of a teaspoon. Wipe the spoon between colours with a rag.

Gently press and turn the tube in the paint, so that the string becomes coated.

Other ideas
Christmas decorations
Sprinkle glitter onto the wet paint and shake off the excess. When it is dry, cut out shapes to make decorations.

String patterns
Make your own printing blocks by arranging some string on a piece of glued cardboard. Press your string pattern into some paint and then use it to make prints.

rag

4 ready-mix paints

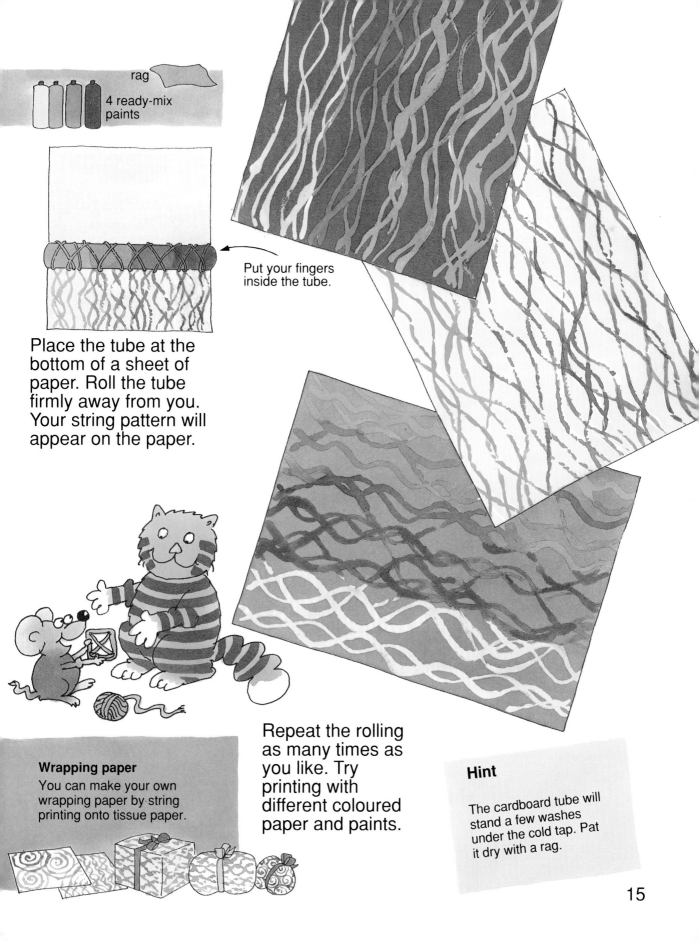

Put your fingers inside the tube.

Place the tube at the bottom of a sheet of paper. Roll the tube firmly away from you. Your string pattern will appear on the paper.

Repeat the rolling as many times as you like. Try printing with different coloured paper and paints.

Wrapping paper

You can make your own wrapping paper by string printing onto tissue paper.

Hint

The cardboard tube will stand a few washes under the cold tap. Pat it dry with a rag.

15

Autumn leaves

You will need:  large cardboard box

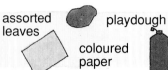 assorted leaves

playdough

coloured paper

dark coloured ready-mix paint

plastic round-ended knife

plastic scrubbing brush

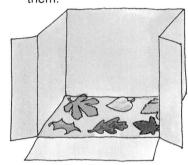

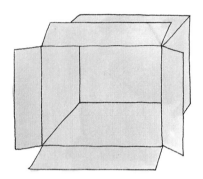

An adult should do the cutting.

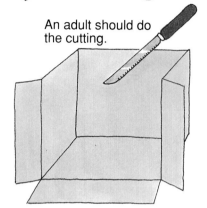

If the leaves don't lie flat stick some playdough under them.

Lay a cardboard box onto one of its long sides. Open out its flaps.

Use a breadknife to cut off the top of the box, as shown.

Lay a sheet of coloured paper inside the box. Arrange some leaves on top of the paper.

Pour some paint into the dish and mix it with a little water. The paint should be quite runny.

Dip a scrubbing brush into the dish and gently shake off the excess paint.

Hints

• It is a good idea to let your child practise drawing the knife across the brush before any paint is applied.

• Take extra care when spatter painting to cover surfaces and wear overalls.

plastic spoon

breadknife

water

plastic or polystyrene dish (slightly longer than the scrubbing brush)

Other ideas

Make lots of single leaf shapes in different colours. Cut them out leaving a thick border of spatter paint. Make a leaf collage by gluing your shapes onto a sheet of paper.

Hold the brush in front of a leaf. Draw the blade of a plastic knife sharply towards you across the bristles.

Move the brush around as you spatter each leaf and the surrounding paper.

Try spatter painting with other flat shapes, such as keys, torn pieces of paper or small flat shells.

Keep the paper flat until the paint has dried. Then lift off the leaves. You

will see the shapes of the leaves surrounded by spattered paint.

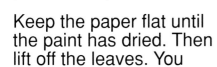

17

Marmalade cat

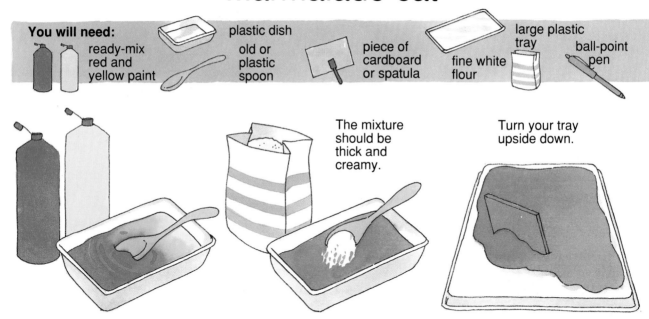

You will need:
ready-mix red and yellow paint · plastic dish · old or plastic spoon · piece of cardboard or spatula · fine white flour · large plastic tray · ball-point pen

The mixture should be thick and creamy.

Turn your tray upside down.

Pour red and yellow paint into a plastic dish. Mix the colours to make a bright orange.

Stir in some fine white flour to make a mixture of about one part flour to three parts paint.

Tip the paint onto the base of a large plastic tray. Spread it evenly and thinly with a piece of cardboard or a spatula.

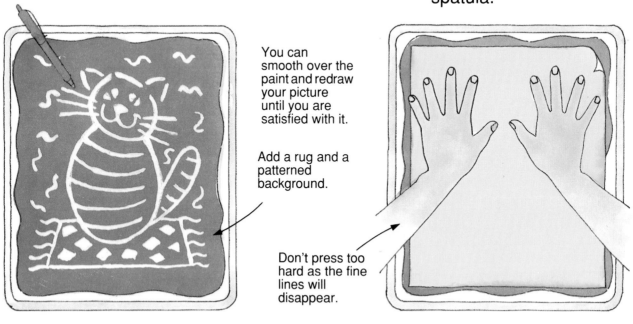

You can smooth over the paint and redraw your picture until you are satisfied with it.

Add a rug and a patterned background.

Don't press too hard as the fine lines will disappear.

Draw your cat into the paint using your fingers for the broad lines, and a ball-point pen for the thin lines.

Wash and dry your hands. Then lay a sheet of paper over the paint and, using the flat of your hands, smooth it very gently.

18

sheet of orange or yellow paper

soap and water

towel

PVA glue

brush for glue

Hint

If you don't have a plastic tray use a smooth kitchen working surface. Afterwards, remove the paint with newspaper before washing.

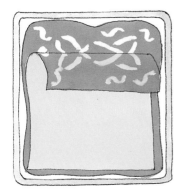

Lift up the top two corners of the paper and slowly peel it back. Be careful not to drag the paint.

Other ideas

Multi-coloured print

Try spreading two or three colours on the tray to make a multi-coloured print.

Window decoration

Make a print on a piece of tissue paper.

Lay a piece of ordinary paper on top of the tissue to prevent it tearing as you smooth it down. When dry, hang it by a window so the light shines through.

Leave the print to dry completely. You can varnish your print by painting it with PVA glue. The glue will be transparent when dry.

Wash the tray immediately after use. Remove any remaining stains with kitchen cleaner.

Magic colours

You will need:

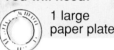 1 large paper plate

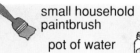 pink, yellow, green and blue ready-mix paints

 4 paint pots

small household paintbrush

pot of water

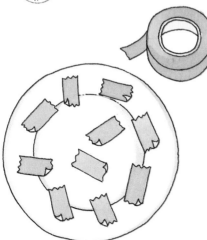

Tear off ten pieces of masking tape, each about 3cm (1in) long. Stick them on a paper plate leaving a corner sticking up.

In paint pots, mix each colour paint with some water. The paint should be fairly runny.

Brush pink paint over the plate and the pieces of tape. Allow the paint to dry.

Hints

• You can also use polystyrene plates.

• Speed the drying process by placing the plate in a microwave oven. Leave it on a high setting for one minute.

• When choosing your own colours always start with light shades and go on to darker colours.

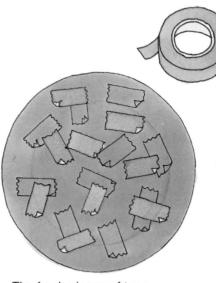

The fresh pieces of tape can overlap the painted pieces but don't cover them completely.

Stick another eight to ten pieces of tape onto the pink paint.

Cover the whole plate with yellow paint and set it aside to dry.

20

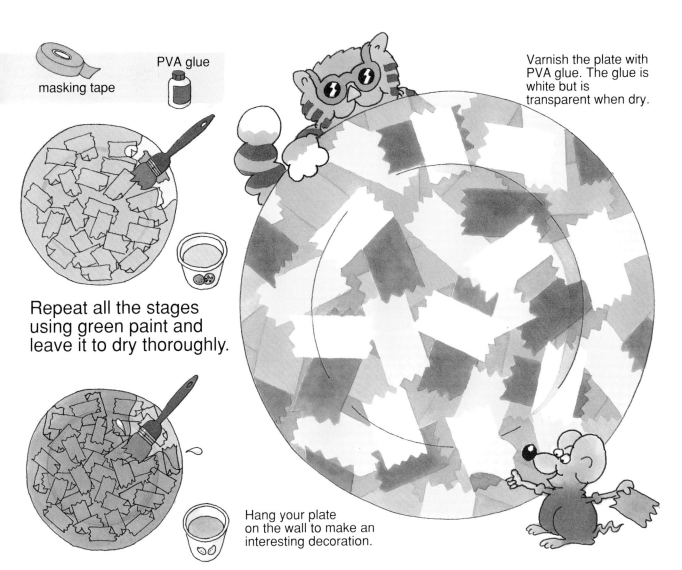

masking tape

PVA glue

Varnish the plate with PVA glue. The glue is white but is transparent when dry.

Repeat all the stages using green paint and leave it to dry thoroughly.

Hang your plate on the wall to make an interesting decoration.

Tape the plate again in the same way and paint it blue. Then set it aside until dry.

Peel the pieces of tape away to reveal the colours underneath. You

don't have to remove all the pieces if you find a pattern you like.

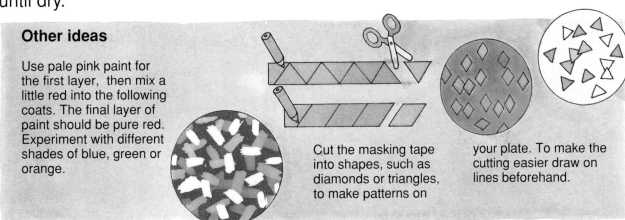

Other ideas

Use pale pink paint for the first layer, then mix a little red into the following coats. The final layer of paint should be pure red. Experiment with different shades of blue, green or orange.

Cut the masking tape into shapes, such as diamonds or triangles, to make patterns on

your plate. To make the cutting easier draw on lines beforehand.

21

Glowing flowers

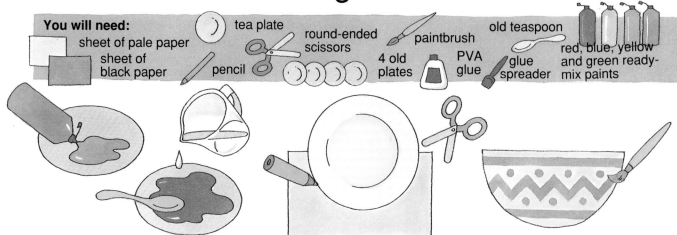

You will need:
sheet of pale paper
sheet of black paper
pencil
tea plate
round-ended scissors
4 old plates
paintbrush
PVA glue
old teaspoon
glue spreader
red, blue, yellow and green ready-mix paints

Pour paint onto four plates. Use one plate for each colour. Mix a little water into the paint and then spread with a teaspoon.

Place a tea plate half onto a piece of pale paper. Draw around the rim of the plate and cut out a bowl shape.

Paint a pattern on the bowl and leave it to dry.

You can dip the twists into two colours for an interesting effect.

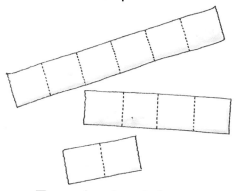

Tear six-sheet, four-sheet and two-sheet lengths of white toilet tissue. You will need about 18 lengths.

To make the flowers, fold the six- and four-sheet lengths of paper in half and then in half again. Twist lightly into rolls, as shown.

Roll the paper twists lightly in the paint. Then dip them quickly into a bowl of warm water and allow them to drip for a few seconds.

Other ideas
Family of snails

Blossom tree

Lady's hat

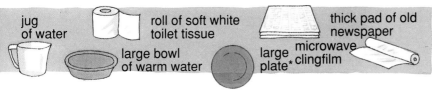

jug of water

roll of soft white toilet tissue

thick pad of old newspaper

large bowl of warm water

large plate*

microwave clingfilm

Bring the two ends together.

Pinch it at each end to make a leaf shape.

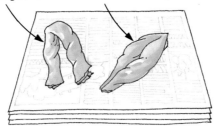

Coil the twists onto a thick pad of newspaper. Press the paper lightly so that a little water seeps out and the colour runs.

For the leaves, fold the two-sheet lengths of paper only once before twisting. Dip the twists into green paint and then the water. Shape them, as above.

Lay the flowers and leaves on a large plate covered with clingfilm. Place the plate in a microwave oven and cook on a high setting for ten minutes, or until they are dry.

Hints

• You can dry the leaves and flowers in a conventional oven. Place them on a baking tray lined with kitchen foil. They will take half an hour to an hour to dry in a moderate oven.

• For this project, you will need to cover surfaces with lots of newspaper and wear waterproof aprons.

Glue the bowl onto black paper. Arrange the flowers with the largest in the centre, filling in the gaps with leaves and smaller flowers. Glue them into place. Leave your picture to dry.

* Only use a plate recommended for microwave use.

Space bubble collage

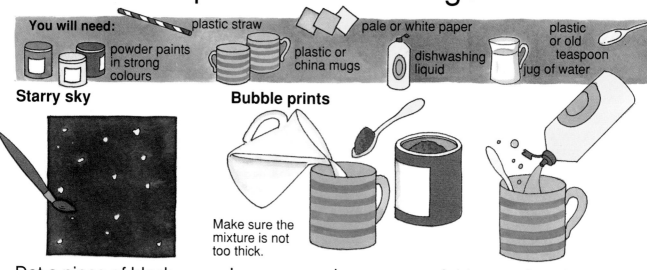

Starry sky

Dot a piece of black paper with white paint to make a starry sky. Set aside to dry.

Bubble prints

Make sure the mixture is not too thick.

In a mug, make up some powder paint following the makers' instructions. The mug should be a third full.

Add a good squirt of dishwashing liquid and stir well with a teaspoon.

Warning

Before you begin, make sure your child can blow through the straw rather than suck.

Stir the straw round to make more bubbles.

Place a straw in the mug and blow until the bubbles rise above the rim.

Lay a piece of paper over the bubbles and press lightly. Lift off the paper without 'dragging' it. Allow it to dry.

Caterpillar

Overlap cut-out bubble prints to make a long caterpillar. Glue the shape onto some paper and paint on its eyes and feet.

Try some different coloured paper and paints. You could also print one colour on top of another for an unusual effect.

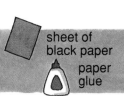 sheet of black paper

paper glue

paints (including white)

 round-ended scissors

paintbrush

pencil

round lids and bottle tops

Planets

Cut out the bubble prints. These are your planets. Draw round lids or bottle tops to make smaller planets.

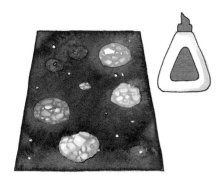

Glue the circles onto the starry background.

Hints

• You can use ready-mix paints for the bubble prints but they do not work as well.

• You could also make a starry sky by spatter painting (see page 17).

You could glue on a painted, cut-out alien and spaceship.

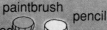

Dip your thumb into paint and print meteors.

Add spot-and-wipe comets (see page 3).

Dazzling snail trail

You will need: red, green, yellow and blue ready-mix paints • 4 paint pots • 4 old or plastic teaspoons • tablespoon • fine white flour • saucepan • water

An adult should do the cooking.

Place one mug of white flour and three mugs of water into a saucepan. Whisk the mixture until it is smooth.

Place the saucepan on the heat and stir the mixture with a wooden spoon until it is thick. Leave it to cool.

Put a good tablespoon of the paste into each of four paint pots.

Add one colour paint to each pot and stir with a teaspoon. The mixture should feel thick and creamy.

Place the icing bag inside a tall plastic tumbler letting the top of the bag overlap the rim.

Drop in heaped teaspoons of the paint mixture, alternating the colours until the bag is half full.

Hints

- Practise piping on a piece of scrap paper before you start.

- Try different-sized nozzles to change the effect.

- You can use the flour and water paste as a glue.

- If the paint stains the icing bag, soak it in sterilising liquid.

This paint takes a long time to dry. Leave it in a warm room or hang it up with pegs - the paint won't run.

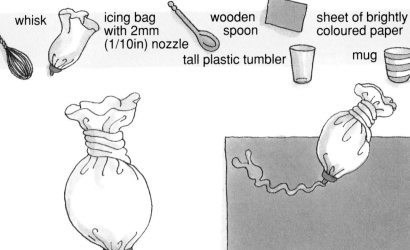

whisk icing bag with 2mm (1/10in) nozzle wooden spoon sheet of brightly coloured paper

tall plastic tumbler mug

Paint some paper plates a bright colour. Leave them to dry and then pipe a pattern.

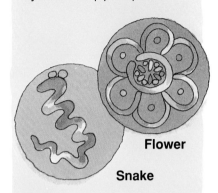

Flower

Snake

Butterfly

Clown

Lift the bag out of the tumbler and gently shake the paint down. Now twist the top lightly.

Squeezing gently, move the bag slowly over a sheet of paper. Make a snail in a top corner. Add horns and a shell.

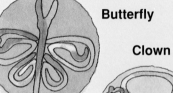

Starting from the snail's tail squeeze a loopy trail all over the

paper. Watch it change colour as you pipe.

27

Animal menagerie

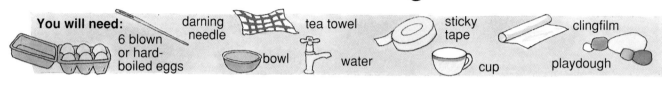

You will need: 6 blown or hard-boiled eggs, darning needle, tea towel, bowl, water, sticky tape, cup, clingfilm, playdough

To blow an egg

Wash the egg under running cold water and dry it gently on a tea towel.

Fix a piece of sticky tape on both ends of the egg.

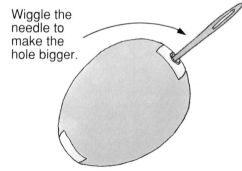

Wiggle the needle to make the hole bigger.

Firmly push a darning needle, through the sticky tape, into the widest end of the egg.

Hold the egg over a bowl and pierce the opposite end. Wiggle the needle to break up the yolk. Peel off the tape.

Now blow hard through the top hole of the egg until its contents are forced out of the bottom*.

Hold the egg at a slant with the larger hole at the top and rinse under the tap. Pat it with a tea towel and leave it to dry before painting.

Boiling eggs

You can also paint boiled eggs. To boil an egg, place it in a pan of cold water and bring it to the boil.

Boil for 15 minutes and then place the pan under cold running water to cool the egg quickly.

* You can save and use the egg contents.

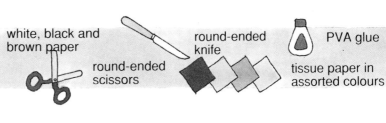

paints · thick and thin paintbrushes · white, black and brown paper · round-ended scissors · round-ended knife · PVA glue · tissue paper in assorted colours

To paint an egg

Allow the egg 'bodies' to dry before adding ears, tails and so on.

Lay some clingfilm over an upturned cup. Press a piece of playdough on top and firmly position your egg on it. Turn the cup as you paint.

Begging puppy

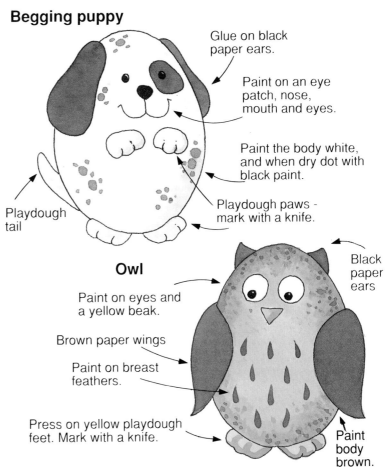

Glue on black paper ears.

Paint on an eye patch, nose, mouth and eyes.

Paint the body white, and when dry dot with black paint.

Playdough tail

Playdough paws - mark with a knife.

Owl

Paint on eyes and a yellow beak.

Brown paper wings

Paint on breast feathers.

Press on yellow playdough feet. Mark with a knife.

Black paper ears

Paint body brown.

Hints

● Large eggs are easier than small eggs to handle and paint.

● If you don't have any playdough you can use marzipan.

● If you don't have the right colour playdough, knead in some ready-mix paint or paint it the right colour.

Little grey mouse

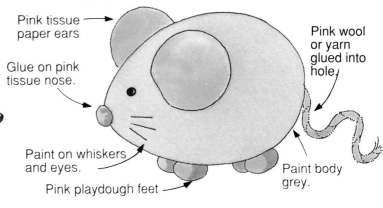

Pink tissue paper ears

Glue on pink tissue nose.

Pink wool or yarn glued into hole.

Paint on whiskers and eyes.

Pink playdough feet

Paint body grey.

Continued on next page.

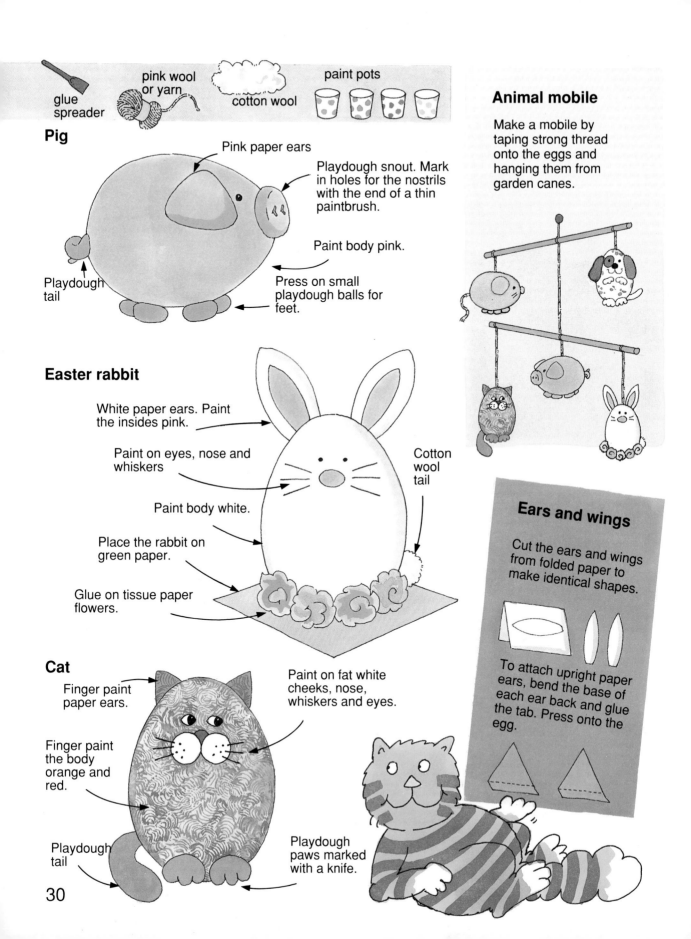

glue spreader

pink wool or yarn

cotton wool

paint pots

Pig

Pink paper ears

Playdough snout. Mark in holes for the nostrils with the end of a thin paintbrush.

Paint body pink.

Playdough tail

Press on small playdough balls for feet.

Easter rabbit

White paper ears. Paint the insides pink.

Paint on eyes, nose and whiskers

Paint body white.

Place the rabbit on green paper.

Glue on tissue paper flowers.

Cotton wool tail

Cat

Finger paint paper ears.

Finger paint the body orange and red.

Playdough tail

Paint on fat white cheeks, nose, whiskers and eyes.

Playdough paws marked with a knife.

Animal mobile

Make a mobile by taping strong thread onto the eggs and hanging them from garden canes.

Ears and wings

Cut the ears and wings from folded paper to make identical shapes.

To attach upright paper ears, bend the base of each ear back and glue the tab. Press onto the egg.

30

Witch's tree

You will need:
 ready-mix paints including blue and black — thin plastic straw, 2 sheets of typing paper, black paper — paintbrush — round-ended scissors — paint pots — sponge — water — glue stick

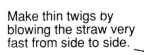

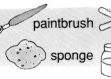

Make thin twigs by blowing the straw very fast from side to side.

Warning
Before you start, make sure your child can blow rather than suck through a straw.

Mix some blue paint and water in a paint pot. Dip a damp sponge into the runny blue paint. Wipe the sponge across a sheet of white paper to make a streaky sky. Leave it to dry.

Pour some large blobs of runny black paint near the centre of the paper. Join the blobs and make a tree shape by blowing hard through a straw. Allow the paint to dry.

Hint

Make sure the blue sky is dry otherwise the black paint will sink in. Absorbent paper is unsuitable for this project.

Other ideas

Make a bright green jungle tree with creepers. Add thumb-print leaves and glue on painted cut-out animals and flowers.

Paint and cut out a witch, owl, cat, cauldron and a moon and then glue them onto your picture. Mount the witch's tree onto a black piece of paper.

Have a paint race with a friend. See who is first to chase their paint from one end of a piece of paper to the other.

Parents' notes

It is well worth spending a little time preparing your painting area. If possible, it is a good idea to work near a sink. Cover work surfaces and surrounding areas with old newspaper, and wear aprons or paint overalls. Have plenty of rags around for wiping brushes, hands and small spills.

Spills

Try to mop up any paint or water spills immediately to avoid any falls on slippery surfaces. If a large quantity of liquid is spilled, soak up the excess with an absorbent cloth then blot gently with another cloth. Remember some paint can stain; it is probably best to follow the manufacturers' instructions if paint is spilled.

Drying and displaying

Paintings will dry more quickly if you lay them on a cake rack, in an airing cupboard or by a sunny window. If you really want to speed up the drying process, place your painting in an oven set on a low temperature.

Displaying your child's work well will add to the pleasure of painting. Mount your picture by sticking it onto a larger piece of paper. Spend some time choosing a colour which will make the most of your child's work.

Colour mixing

The basic colours you will need are: black, white, yellow, blue, green and red. You can mix green but the resulting colour is not so bright.

Below is a colour mixing chart so you can experiment with different combinations.

Blue + red = brown

Blue + pink = purple/mauve

Blue + yellow= green

Yellow + red or pink = orange

Red + green = warm shades of brown

Green + yellow = acid green

Green + blue = dark leaf green

Basic materials

Paints

Paints should be non-toxic and water soluble. Ready-mix paints are suitable for many projects and can easily be thinned down. You can buy ready-mix paints from large newsagents*, art supply stores and shops selling educational aids and toys. Powder and poster paints are also widely available. Don't forget to read the manufacturer's cleaning advice before use.

Paint pots

These are sometimes necessary for mixing and thinning paint. Use old yogurt pots or similar containers to keep from buying them. Mix large amounts of paint in plastic ice cream tubs.

Brushes

A small household paintbrush is useful for painting large areas. You also need thick and thin children's brushes.

Glue

PVA (polyvinyl acetate)** can be used as a glue or brushed over paint to varnish it. It is white but dries transparent. PVA glue also adds strength to painted work and protects surfaces. Glue sticks are clean to use and the glue is easily directed.

Paper

Packs of coloured play paper can be bought quite cheaply. Cartridge and typing paper are less absorbent and are suitable for certain projects. Breakfast cereal boxes make a good source of thin cardboard.

*hobby shops (U.S.) ** all-purpose glue (U.S.)